Will AND Squill

Emma Chichester Clark

🍃 **Carolrhoda Books, Inc.** ◦ **Minneapolis**

for

Janice Thomson

First American edition published in 2006 by Carolrhoda Books, Inc.

Copyright © 2005 by Emma Chichester Clark

Originally published in 2005 by Andersen Press Ltd., London, England.

Carolrhoda Books, Inc.
A division of Lerner Publishing Group
241 First Avenue North
Minneapolis, MN 55401 U.S.A.

Website address: www.lernerbooks.com

Library of Congress Cataloging-in-Publication Data

Chichester Clark, Emma.
    Will and Squill / by Emma Chichester Clark.— 1st American ed.
      p. cm.
    Summary: Young Will and Squill the squirrel manage to stay best friends despite
a few tests to the strength of their friendship.
    ISBN-13: 978–1–57505–936–5 (lib. bdg. : alk. paper)
    ISBN-10: 1–57505–936–3 (lib. bdg. : alk. paper)
    [1. Babies—Fiction. 2. Squirrels—Fiction. 3. Best friends—Fiction.
    4. Friendship—Fiction. 5. Stories in rhyme.] I. Title.
PZ8.3.C4327Wil 2006
[E]—dc22   2005015582

Printed and bound in Singapore
1 2 3 4 5 6 – OS – 11 10 09 08 07 06

This is how Will met Squill,
and Squill met Will.
They were little.
Little Will and
little Squill.

"Oh, no darling!"
cried Will's mother.

"Oh, no darling!"
cried Squill's
mother.

" . . . awful dirty squirrel!"
said Will's mother.
" . . . awful dirty baby!"
said Squill's mother.

But Squill wanted Will,
and Will wanted Squill.

With Squill, Will
took his first steps.

With Will, Squill
took his first swim.

Squill grew. Will grew.

Will!

Squill!

Will's parents gave Will
lots of fluffy toys,
but he only wanted Squill.

Squill's parents gave Squill
lots of little brothers
and sisters, but
he only wanted Will.

Will and Squill had
plenty of things to do.
"Swing!" said Squill.
"I will if you will!" said Will.
"I squill!" said Squill.

They had plenty of things to play.
"Squill will if Will will!" sang Squill.
"Will will if Squill will!" sang Will.

And they had plenty of things to try.
"Will you try some spaghetti, Squill?" asked Will.
"I will, Will," said Squill. "I love squilletti!"
"And wilkshake!" said Will.

but sometimes,
in the same place.

"Goodnight, Squill,"
said Will.
"Goodnight, Will,"
said Squill.

Then one day,
Will's parents
had a surprise
for him.

"Oh!" cried Will.

"Your very own kitten!"
they said.
"Here, little kitty!"
said Will.

"Good little kitty,"
said Will.

"Look! She's dancing!"
said Will.

"Smart little kitty!"
said Will.

"Come on, kitty! Catch, little kitty!" said Will.
"Roly-poly, tickly tummy!" said Will.

"Silly little kitty!"
hissed Squill.

Yeeoow!

"Hey, Squill!"
cried Will.
"Stop that
right now!"

"Poor little kitty!" said Will.
"Go away!" said Will to Squill.
"I will!" said Squill.

But . . . the kitten didn't really like bouncing.
And the kitten didn't really like soccer.

The kitten didn't really seem to want to do
anything . . . except sleep . . .

and sleep.

The kitten wasn't really much fun after all.

Will missed Squill.

He missed everything about Squill.

"What's the matter, Will?"
asked his parents.
"I miss Squill," said Will.

"Where is Squill? Will
he ever come back?"
wondered Will.

And then,
Will saw Squill!

"Squill!" said Will.
"Will!" said Squill.
"You look silly!" said Will.
"I feel squilly!" said Squill.

"I really miss you, Squill," said Will.
"I really miss you, Will," said Squill.

"Will you say sorry?"
asked Squill.
"I will if you will,"
said Will.
"I squill if you squill,"
said Squill.
"I'm sorry!" said Will.
"I'm sorry!" said Squill.

"Well, I'm not sorry!"
said the little girl.
"Can I play with your kitten?"

"Yes!" said Will.
"*Definitely* yes!"
said Squill.

"Good little kitty!
Time for a nap!"
said the little girl.
"*Yes!*" purred the kitten.

Squill's parents saw
and Will's parents saw
that where there's a Will
there's a Squill,
and where there's a Squill
there's a Will,
and it was better that way.

"I hope we'll always be friends," said Will.

"Squill will if Will will!" sang Squill.

"Will will if Squill will!" sang Will.

"So we will!" said Squill.

"Yes, we squill!" said Will.

And they were.

Forever.